LittLe CriTTer's®
THE PICNIC

BY
MERCER MAYER

*To Jamie,
Nevis &
Alburn*

A Golden Book • New York
Western Publishing Company, Inc., Racine, Wisconsin 53404

What a nice day
for a picnic.

Too many cars.

Too many critters.

We will find
a better spot.

This is a
good spot.

Too many cows.

I know
another spot.

What a good spot
for a picnic.

Too bad.
We have
to go.

That looks like
a good spot.

This is a
good spot.

Too many bees.

This is not
a good spot.

But this is.

Too many bears.

We can have
a picnic there.

Hello!
Is anyone
home?

Too many bats.

It is too wet
up here.

I know a
good spot.

This looks like
a good spot.

What a good spot
for a picnic!

What a nice day
for a picnic,
after all.